The death of the sentence

helicopter lullaby and *alive* previously published in *Orbis*.

Death Certificate, My novel, The only novel I could ever write, The novel I could never write, The novel that wrote itself previously published in *Sarasvati*.

Publisher: Independently published.
Publication date: July 2020

ISBN: 9798655432918

Contents

My novel

after Raymond Carver

The novel that made me laugh,
the novel that made me cry,
the novel I lost at the airport,
the novel I ripped to shreds,
the novel that disappeared without a trace,
the novel that grew out of all proportion,
the novel I left in the hotel room,
the novel that fell out of the sky,
the novel everyone forgot,
the novel I burnt in the fireplace,
the novel that ruined my life,
the novel that everybody remembers,
the novel I threw out the window,
the novel that crushed civilization,
the novel that inspired revolution,
the novel that propped up my coffee table,
the novel that fell into a black hole,
the novel I buried in the garden,
the novel that exploded,
the novel that began with a whimper,
the novel that found me love,
the novel that predicted my death,
the novel that announced my birth,
the novel that drove me crazy,
the novel that brought me hope,
the novel that saved my life,
the novel I will always remember,
the only novel I could ever write,
the novel I could never write,
the novel that wrote itself.
My novel.

The poem that brought me hope

Shine. Shine bright.

Frighten the shadows with your burning. Drop from the sky in dandelions and sunflowers.

Be bold. Be courageous. Topple your enemies with your passion. Spread peace with your presence.

Shine in the petals, shine in the leaves, shine in the air, shine in every particle of dust, shine in the suffocating crowds, shine in the traffic jams, shine in the offices, shine in the airports, shine in the shopping malls. Shine in the dark.

Yours is the light I must follow.

Shine for me.

Balancing Act

The sea washed around the sandpits where we played. Dinosaurs stalked the corridors while Mrs B pointed her finger at us repeating *the fur will fly, the fur will fly*. Parents cartwheeled and capered at summer sports days. We struggled with our six and seven times tables as Mr B aimed his shoe at our elaborate Lego castles. Could anything be louder than our bat screeches in the dining hall? Nativities sparkled on the tightropes of our Christmases. We sat on the floor in morning assemblies watching the headmistress performing tricks on her unicycle. I always wondered how she never fell off.

helicopter lullaby

you can't grow a helicopter overnight

grow, helicopter, grow
grow in the moonlight

gather your frenzy, escape
from your shell

a bluebottle on acid
a dragon unleashed

make sloth your enemy, explode
from the trees

sever your mother's web
and skate on the wind

Quote from an interview with a NATO commander in Afghanistan

(2006)

alive

a poem for two voices

shocked to find alive   *to find alive*
in a sack of potatoes she bought   *she bought*
at the market   *the market*

thought to have come   *to have come*
from a farm in France   *a farm in France*

alerted the neighbours   *the neighbours*
who in turn called the police   *called the police*

detonated on Wednesday   *on Wednesday*

it is believed to be a type   *a type*
used by the US Army during World War II   *used during World War II*

Olga Mauriello, from a small town near Naples,   *near Naples*
put the potatoes into water to peel them   *to peel them*
when she discovered   *she discovered*

'If I hadn't felt its weight   *felt its weight*
I wouldn't even have realized'   *even have realized*
she told Reuters news agency[1]   *Reuters news agency*

---

[1] Thu 1st March 2007

Pushbike Passion

Large Puncture Tyre Repair Kit with Tyre Levers
Contains: 24xPatches, 15g adhesive, 2xTyre Levers
Sandpaper, Chalk, Marker Crayon

a puncture, a wound
I bleed, I cannot breathe
sinking, sinking
I stagger up again

gentle track to my dusty
heart, bless a rusty nail to protect me
for who by caring, bleeding, drowning
will end this road?

The only novel I could ever write
                                    will be written by stealth
In stolen moments, walking in corridors, waiting for lifts
A book of fragments, episodes, anecdotes, jottings,
ramblings, scramblings
No plot to speak of, a motley assortment of characters,
random word jumbles to amuse the brain
What sort of a novel is that?
The only novel I could ever write.

The poem everyone forgot

An absence. A shadow. A flicker of batwings
What was that you thought you heard?
On the edge of awareness, the space beyond thought,
the poem skips and jumps, flitting from mind
to mind, carefree. Who are we to halt it?
Is this the poem that can stop Death in his tracks?
None of us can force it to drown in memory's quicksand
Perhaps you will hear it again one day and marvel at its beauty
Just make sure you tell it to somebody first.

Z is for Zero

Carbon dating shows an ancient Indian manuscript has the earliest recorded origin of the zero symbol [BBC Sept 2017] Bakhshali manuscript, 3rd-4th century

I remember travelling to Ground Zero in New York a few years after the World Trade Centre attack. So strange to think I had visited the Twin Towers in 1981, how iconic they had been. Their destruction cast those events into negative time, the time before their fall. What about those other ground zeroes, Hiroshima and Nagasaki? Not to mention all the nuclear tests since then. Does anybody count these zeroes as a measure of human folly?

Nature has its own ground zeroes: volcanoes, diseases, earthquakes, meteor strikes. All these zeroes mount up. On a galactic scale, the Big Bang is the ultimate zero. And our galaxy, the Milky Way, has a zero spot, a supermassive black hole at its centre, as do other large galaxies, each of them spinning around their zero spots, careful to avoid that dangerous event horizon, beyond which everything will be transformed in the singularity. While, here on Earth, humanity waits for its own technological and spiritual singularity, hoping this will reach us before we perish under the weight of all our zeroes.

The Multifarious Moons of Saturn

Aegaeon. Anthe. Atlas. Calypso. Daphnis. Dione. Enceladus. Epimetheus. Helene. Hyperion. Iapetus. Janus. Methone. Mimas. Pallene. Pan. Pandora. Phoebe. Polydeuces. Prometheus. Rhea. Telesto. Tethys. Titan.

Like a giant game of solar billiards, huge lumps of rock hurtling through space around the Copernican compass of Saturn himself. Their gravitational forces conspire and combine to keep those magical rings in place and visible from afar, blocks of orbital ice continually colliding to reveal new crystal surfaces.

And they've only named fifty-three of them.

Aegir; Albiorix; Bebhionn; Bergelmir; Bestla; Erriapus; Farbauti; Fenrir; Fornjot; Greip; Hati; Hyrrokkin.

If I opened a bar, I would call it *The Multifarious Moons of Saturn*. A different cocktail for each lonely satellite.

Ijiraq - Jarnsaxa - Kari - Kiviuq - Loge - Mundilfari - Narvi - Paaliaq - Siarnaq - Skathi - Skoll - Surtur - Suttungr - Tarqeq - Tarvos - Thrymr - Ymir.

And if, at the end of my days, I never step foot on Titan, Mundilfari or any of the other moons of Saturn? Well, at least I've felt the attraction of their planetary dance and raised a glass in their lunar honour.

The novel I could never write

How can I begin? The fact is *beginning* implies an idea or plan where I have none. This is the blankest of slates. All I have is the germ of a concept. The merest speck.

The human brain is a marvel! So many layers of images and words sparking trains of association that travel through the labyrinths of our thoughts until they start to turn upon each other.

So what is the novel about? I sit in the storehouse of my ideas and stew in the heat of my imagination. Relax. This is the core, the fire and it is invention, inexhaustible human invention: languages; lists; secret words; flights of fancy; borogroves; bandersnatches; ice palaces; mind palaces; greenhouses; observatories; museums; galleries and telescopes; robots; computers; Mastermind; gyroscopes; compasses and astrolabes; screwdrivers and kaleidoscopes; colour wheels and plastics; Bakelite; nylon stockings and space rockets; fireworks and steam engines; cars and bicycles; ships and submarines; bathyscaphes and orbiting space stations; cable-cars; mountain-climbing and ski-jumps; Morse code; telegrams; telephones and radar; the CERN laboratory; Tibetan wind-prayers and Japanese haiku; lighthouses; skyscrapers; electricity pylons and undersea cables; The Eiffel Tower; The Forth Bridge; ironworks, suspension bridges; trains and railways. And so, inevitably, my thoughts start to tumble upon themselves.

the sound of one poet wrestling

sumo, clouds fading
zoom, a chasm, a schism
doom, a cosmic museum
giant mushrooms, fearsome bosom
a crown of jasmine blossom

At the "Snow and Roses"
after Louis MacNiece

Walk in and I can hear birdsong. Or is it whale-music? On all sides are stacks of anthologies, bundles of collections and showers of pamphlets. Think of a poet and a book is in my hand. Feel sad for a moment and a luminous sonnet fills my heart. Walking through the stacks is a reverie, there are clocks and astrolabes, wind-chimes and starcharts, jars of gobstoppers and mint humbugs, sprigs of jasmine and thyme. One corner has snowglobes of the bookshop, with the pink letters of its sign shining against white. I pick one up and shake it to see myself walking in through the door.

The Poet's Duty

My duty is to fail every day
Try to write a poem / Fail
Try again / Fail a second time
Pull myself up by my bootstraps / Fail because I am weak
Look to the past for inspiration / Fail because I am confused
Summon all my energy and throw myself at that elusive brick
wall / Taste the bitterness of failure
Throw my pens and books to the floor / Feel the relative
comfort of failure
Consider each of my previous attempts and try again / Fail
with dignity
Remember why I am a poet / Fail with honour
Only when I have failed for the last time can I realise what
success looks like
I am ready to write my poem.

The novel that wrote itself

It started with an itch. A scratch. A twitch. *I want to launch myself into space, my selfshot to nothingness.* I used to wake up in the middle of the night in a cold sweat, mumbling to myself. *Lonely selfships in the selfdrome, who is the master and who is the slave?* Uncontaminated by reality's tentacles, it erupted into castles, mansions, fortresses, spaceships, mazes, caverns, tunnels, corridors, mirrors and windows, windows, countless windows. *Flying high, my selfship cut loose, free from all the boneheads but still a slave to my selfhood, I need to plumb the deep vacuum of consciousness.* Taking over my life, it shouldered me out of the picture, grew horns and wings until it became the shipmate to my loneliness, my skullshot to happiness. The splashdown came all too soon and I was cast adrift, victim of a cruel selfmate. I resumed my everyday existence, but the novel remains on the shelf, the unforgettable snapshot.

The Dystopia Factory

for Hugo and Nebula

spaceship rampant, renegade spaceship
spaceship spectral, derelict spaceship
spaceship sentient, pot-bellied spaceship
take me off this planet and fly me across the universe
through asteroid belts, robot mutinies, collapsing empires
from warp factor to wormhole, from hyperspace to inner
space
through android conspiracies, colliding moons, interstellar
battlegrounds
from ion drive to dimension jump, from black hole to white
dwarf
through angry gods, decaying megastructures and frozen
timebubbles
spaceship drive me home

Space Hymn XVII

build yourself a starship
a century of tears, a mountain
of fingernails, a prayer-book
of leaves

cultivate a crew of uncut
willows, rooted to the floor
your map will be a sparrow's nest
hawkmoth wings your door

untie the tangled light-
years, tremble as they fall
scatter dust behind you
is this the human dawn?

How to unwrite your novel

Start with the opening sentence. Demolish it. Starve the syllables of meaning.

Start with the protagonist. Steal their motivation. Find each character and give them an irresistible reason to die.

Start with the ending. Drown it. Unwind the plot and crumple it in your hands.

Start with the title. Bury it. Scramble the chapter headings and cook them up for beginnings.

Start with the inspiration. Strangle it. Dance a jig of gratitude as it disappears into nothing.

Start with the opening sentence.

Death Certificate

I would love to write a first collection
a screenplay
a political drama
a western
a spy story
a war epic
a detective novel
an historical novel
a fantasy epic
a bestselling contemporary novel
a SF classic
my autobiography
my obituary
my epitaph

I would love to write for the hell of it
for the sheer pleasure of it
for money
for a living
to my younger self
to my older self
to my unknown self
to lost friends
to new friends
until the end of my life
until the end of time
in my dreams
forever

How did he die?
Writer's block.

The sentence falls into a black hole

I give you the death of the sentence, witness its falling, vanishing to the point of destruction, what a great life it had, its ability to straddle the void unsurpassed, it could ride the heavens with ease, defying gravity and time to turbocharge our imaginations, once beyond the event horizon its staccato thunderbolts and pizzicato epiphanies can do nothing to save it, sucking, stretching, openings and endings disappearing before our very eyes, it is the end of dust, the swallower of souls, the art and dream of the sentence shining and collapsing into the maw of the black hole, and we are left with nothing but our mem-

Printed in Poland
by Amazon Fulfillment
Poland Sp. z o.o., Wrocław

61884093R00016